KING OF THE PLAYGROUND

By *Phyllis Reynolds Naylor*
Illustrated by Nola Langner Malone

Aladdin Paperbacks

Other Books for Young Readers
by Phyllis Reynolds Naylor

Old Sadie and the Christmas Bear
Keeping a Christmas Secret

First Aladdin Paperbacks edition 1994

Text copyright © 1991 by Phyllis Reynolds Naylor
Illustrations copyright © 1991 by Nola Langner Malone

Aladdin Paperbacks
An imprint of Simon & Schuster Children's Publishing Division
1230 Avenue of the Americas
New York, NY 10020

Printed in Hong Kong
10   9   8   7

Library of Congress Cataloging-in-Publication Data
Naylor, Phyllis Reynolds.
    The King of the Playground / by Phyllis Reynolds Naylor : illustrated by Nola Langner Malone. —
1st Aladdin Books ed.
        p.   cm.
    Summary: With his dad's help, Kevin overcomes his fear of the "King of the Playground" who has
threatened to tie him to the slide, put him in a deep hole, or put him in a cage with bears.
    ISBN 0-689-71802-0
    [1. Bullies–Fiction.   2. Playgrounds–Fiction.]   I. Malone, Nola Langner, ill.   II. Title.
PZ7.N24Ki   1994
[E]–dc20   93-25125

To Henry Charles and his sisters   —PRN

*For Lelia Mandeville
who knows about healing   —NLM*

Kevin put on his Spiderman T-shirt, his Batman underpants, and his jeans with the horseshoe on each pocket. But he didn't feel brave and he didn't feel lucky.

He walked up the street to the playground. He wanted to go down the slide headfirst. But if Sammy was there, he wouldn't go down at all.

Too late. Sammy was there.

"You can't come in!" Sammy said. "I'm King of the Playground!" And he told Kevin what he would do if he saw him on the slide.

Kevin went back home. His father was making soup.

"I thought you went to the playground," said Father.

"Sammy says if I go on the slide, he'll get a rope
and tie me up," Kevin told him. "He says he'll tie
my hands and feet so tight I'll never get loose."

"Wow!" said Father. "Really? And what would you be doing while Sammy was tying you up? Just sitting there?"

Kevin remembered when he tried to put a sweater on their cat.

"I'd be kicking my feet," he said.
"Right," said his dad. "That's one thing you could do."

The next day Kevin went to the playground and got as far as the swings.

"You can't play here!" yelled Sammy, running over. "I'm King of the Swings." And he told Kevin what he would do if he saw him on the swings.

Kevin went home and sat on the porch. Father
was washing his car.
"I thought you were going to the playground,"
Father called.

Kevin shook his head. "Sammy says if I go on the swings, he'll dig a hole and put me in it. He says he'll dig a hole so deep I'll never get out."

Father smiled just a bit. "How long do you think it would take Sammy to dig that hole?"

Kevin remembered when he had helped his father dig holes for fence posts in the backyard. "A long time," he said.

"And what would you be doing while Sammy was digging?"

"I'd be kicking the dirt back in," said Kevin, and smiled a little, too.

"Right," said his dad. "That's one thing you could do."

The next day Kevin went to the playground and tried to climb the monkey bars.

"You can't play here! I'm King of the Monkey Bars!" Sammy shouted, and told Kevin what he would do if he saw him there again.

Kevin went home and climbed up the maple tree.
His father was working in the garden.
"I thought you were going to the playground,"
said Father.

"Sammy says if I climb the monkey bars, he'll
come over to our house and nail all the doors and
windows shut and we'll be trapped forever." Kevin
looked at his father, and they both started to laugh.

"And while Sammy was nailing one door shut,
we could walk out the other," Kevin said.
"Right," said his dad.

The next morning Kevin put on his Spiderman T-shirt, his Batman underpants, and his jeans with the horseshoe on each pocket. He felt only a little bit brave and a little bit lucky.

He walked up the street to the playground. *Thump, thump, thump,* went his heart.

Sammy was sitting by himself in the sandbox. It was a big sandbox, but when Sammy was in it, nobody else wanted to play.

Kevin slowly walked over.
"You can't play here!" Sammy yelled when he
saw him. "I'm King of the Sandbox!"

Kevin put one foot in the box.
"Go home!" Sammy yelled, even louder. "If you
try to play here, I'll put you in a cage with bears in it."

Kevin put his other foot in the sandbox. "Then I'll ride on their backs and teach them tricks," he said.

Sammy stared. "You can't!" he yelled. "They're wild bears!"

"Then I'll squeeze through the cage and escape."

"You can't!" Sammy shouted. "You're too big!"

"Then I'll take magic pills to make me little," said Kevin, beginning to smile. "I'll get through the cage and hide."

"You can't!" Sammy hollered. "I'll run after you
and pick you up and throw you in a trash can."

"Then I'll take magic pills to make me big again,
and I'll drive away in a truck."

"You can't!" bellowed Sammy. "I'll go to the army and get a tank and chase the truck and push it off into the ocean."

"Try it," said Kevin.
Sammy stopped hollering. "What?" he asked.
"Try it," said Kevin, and sat down.

He began digging a tunnel at one end of the
sandbox.

For a moment Sammy didn't say anything at all.
Then *he* began digging a tunnel at *his* end of the
sandbox.

Faster and faster and farther and farther they dug,
until suddenly—*whump!*

They bumped heads right in the middle.

This time Kevin laughed out loud. He wasn't sure, but he thought maybe Sammy was smiling, too.

"I'm going to build the biggest fort in the world," Kevin said, and began digging again.

"Ha!" said Sammy. "It's got to have towers."
"It will," Kevin said.
"It's got to have a drawbridge," said Sammy.
"It will," Kevin said.
"It's got to have a ditch all around," said Sammy.
"It will," Kevin said. "Help me build it?"

"No," Sammy told him.
But he did.